Emily Windsnap's Fin-tastic Friendship Book

Emily Windsnap's Fin-tastic Friendship Book

Liz Kessler

illustrations by Sarah Gibb

CANDLEWICK PRESS

First U.S. edition 2009

ISBN 978-0-7636-3960-0

2   4   6   8   10   9   7   5   3   1

Printed in the United States of America

This book was typeset in Bembo.
The illustrations were done in watercolor.

Candlewick Press
99 Dover Street
Somerville, Massachusetts 02144

visit us at www.candlewick.com

This book belongs to:

Anna Frey

Date:

December, 23, 04

My best friend is:

We've been best friends for

.... *years* .... *months* .... *days*

With excerpts from:

The Tail of Emily Windsnap =

Emily Windsnap and the Monster from the Deep =

Emily Windsnap and the Castle in the Mist =

Contents

PART I

Best Friends

PART II

Friendship and Fun

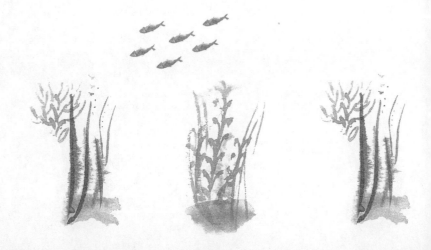

PART III

Underwater Sleepover

PART IV

Beneath the Waves

Hi,
and welcome to my friendship book!

I didn't always have a best friend. At one point, I thought I was so different from everyone else that I'd never have a real friend who I could share all my secrets with, and who would understand me and like me for who I am. And then I met Shona! She made me see that it was OK to be different and that it didn't make me a freak. It made me interesting and cool—and swishy! And she made me realize that even though it's fine not having a best friend, it's so-o-o-o-o-o-o much nicer when you have one.

I happen to think that Shona is the bestest best friend in the world—and I know we'll always be there for each other. Maybe that's how you feel about your best friend, too. If so, you'll love reading this book with your best friend.

You'll be able to find out all sorts of things about each other by analyzing each other's clothes, hairstyles, and handwriting! You can find out why you're such good friends and share your hopes and wishes. You can even create matching tokens to show how important you are to each other, just as Shona and I did with our friendship pebbles.

I hope you and your best friend have as much fun with this book as Shona and I have had splashing in the sea together. Maybe it will lead you to adventures that are just as exciting (although maybe not as scary) as some of ours!

Swishy wishes,

Emily x x x o o o

PART I

Best Friends

I looked up to see her staring at me as though I were something from outer space that had washed up on the beach. I stared back and tried folding my arms, too. I found that if I kept flicking my tail a little, I could stay upright. So I flicked and folded and stared for a little while, and she did the same. Then I noticed the side of her mouth flutter a bit and I felt the dimple below my left eye twitching. A second later, we were both laughing like hyenas.

"What are we laughing at?" I said when I managed to catch my breath.

"I don't know!" she answered — and we both burst out laughing again.

"What's your name?" she said once we'd stopped laughing. "I'm Shona Silkfin."

"Emily," I said. "Emily Windsnap."

All about Emily and Shona

> *Nothing made [Shona] happier than learning a new way to style her hair or get the best shine out of her tail or swim with perfect elegance. I was more interested in shipwreck studies and siren stories.*

Emily and Shona have taken time out from swimming and swishing about in the sea to compile some VIFs (very important facts) about themselves.

EMILY'S VIFs

Full name: Emily Windsnap

Best friend: Shona Silkfin

Schools: Brightport Junior High and
       Allpoints Island School

Height: 4 feet 9 inches

Color of tail: purple and green

Hair color: light brown

Special feature: my legs—when I'm not in the sea

Favorite word: wicked

Age: 12

A Best Friend . . .

is always there for you when you need her.

"We will NOT give up!" Shona said, swimming around in front of my face and lifting my chin just as Mom does when she forces me to listen. "Do you hear me?" she said sternly. "That is not my best friend talking. The one who explores shipwrecks and caves and breaks into prisons to rescue her dad! OK?"

SHONA'S VIFs

Full name: Shona Silkfin

Best friend: Emily Windsnap

Schools: Shiprock School

Allpoints Island School

Height: 4 feet 10 inches

Color of tail: silvery green

Hair color: blond

Special feature: my long, slim tail

Favorite word: swishy

Age: 12

OFFICIAL BEST FRIEND

All about You and Your Best Friend

Now it's your turn. Fill in your VIFs and ask your best friend to fill in hers. Then place photos of yourselves in the frame.

Why don't you visit a photo booth and squeeze in together?

MY VIFs

Name: Anna

Nickname: Hoot

Best friend:

Schools: Southeast

Height: 4 feet 5 inches

Hair color: Very dark brown

Eye color: dark brown

Special feature: run fast

Favorite word: soccer

Age: 9 and 1 month 6 days.

Birthday: December, 23, 04

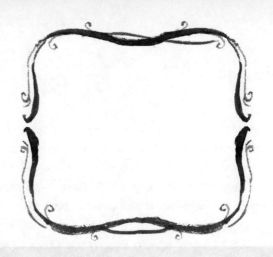

MY BEST FRIEND'S VIFs

Name: Michele

Nickname: Shelly

Best friend: Anna

Schools: Cornell

Height: 5' 9 ½ "

Hair color: Brown

Eye color: Blue

Special feature: funny

Favorite word:

Age: 43

Birthday: 2/20/1970

Friendship Pebbles

Then she scrabbled around among the rocks and picked up a couple of stones. She handed one to me.

"What's this?" I looked at the stone.

"They're friendship pebbles. They mean that we're best friends—if you want to be."

"Of course I want to be!"

"See? They're almost exactly the same." She showed me her pebble. "We each keep ours on us at all times. It means we'll always be there for each other." . . .

I washed my pebble in the water; it went all shiny and smooth. "It's the best present anyone's ever given me."

Swapping friendship tokens is the perfect way to show your best friend how important she is to you. If you want to trade pebbles the way Emily and Shona did, look on the beach, in the park, or in your backyard for the prettiest pebbles you can find. You might be as lucky as Shona was and find two that are almost exactly the same.

If your pebbles are smooth, you could paint them. Why don't you paint your friend's pebble and ask her to paint yours?

You'll need:

> * *nail polish (clear or glittery)*
>
> * *acrylic paints*
>
> * *paintbrushes*

How to do it:

If your pebbles are a pretty color, brush them with clear nail polish to make them glow or glittery nail polish to make them sparkle. Swishy! If not, paint your pebbles with a base coat of light-colored paint.

After the pebbles dry, it's time for the fun part—decorating them! Turn the page for some suggestions.

Suggestions:

* Paint a pattern of brightly
  colored flowers or polka
  dots on the pebbles.

**Remember to
keep your pebbles
somewhere
safe.**

* Paint each other's
  names on them in
  fancy writing.

* What about painting faces
  on the pebbles? You could paint
  self-portraits—or each other.

* If you found your pebbles on the beach,
  keep to a seaside theme by painting shells, fish,
  or mermaids on them.

* Try painting a big *B* on one pebble and a
  big *F* on the other. Bring them together,
  and you'll have *BF* for "Best Friends."

* Paint a picture across both pebbles. When
you're apart, you'll have only half the picture,
but when you're together, you can join your
pebbles like two pieces of a jigsaw puzzle. Start
with pebbles that have the same background
color. Put them side by side to see what shape
they make together. If your pebbles make a
long, thin shape, you could paint a tall tree or
a rainbow on them. If they make a rounder or
squarer shape, you could paint a big yellow sun
or a flower on them.

When your pebbles are perfect, it's time to swap!

Personality Traits

If you could choose just three words to describe
your best friend, what would they be? And which
three words would she choose to describe you?
Look at the list below if you need help coming up
with the words, and write your selections on the
next page. Then see if you can choose three words
for Emily and three words for Shona, too.

* happy
* calm
* quiet
* lively
* shy
* clever
* knowledgeable
* spirited
* imaginative
* mischievous
* reliable

* bubbly
* friendly
* outgoing
* dramatic
* brave
* thoughtful
* active
* inventive
* daydreamer
* kind
* silly

"Emily, I think we need to get back." A fat green angelfish hovered between us, startled eyes staring into ours before it spun around and disappeared into a rocky crevice. "We've seen it now. We're not supposed to be here."

Me:

Happy
Outgoing
BRAVE

My best friend:

Calm
quiet
reliable

Emily:

Clever
Friendly
active

Shona:

Clever
friendly
Silly

11

PERSONALITY PROFILES

Now see if you fit any of the descriptions below
to find out what sort of friend you are.

* If you're **happy, bubbly, friendly, outgoing,
lively, silly, dramatic,** or **mischievous** — you
may be a *Fun-Loving Friend*.

  Fun-loving friends are great company at parties
  and on shopping trips, and they love a good laugh!

* If you're **kind, reliable, calm, friendly, quiet,** or
thoughtful — you may be a *Caring Friend*.

  When someone has a problem, a caring friend
  is just what that person needs. Caring friends
  are good listeners, and they always try to help.

* If you're **lively, brave, spirited, active,** or
mischievous — you may be an *Adventurous
Friend*.

  Adventurous friends can lead you into all sorts of
  crazy situations, which can be fun — and scary, too!

* If you're **shy, thoughtful, imaginative, calm,** or a **daydreamer**—you may be a *Dreamy Friend.*

Dreamy friends need to be shaken awake sometimes, but they are always full of fascinating dreams and schemes.

* If you're **clever, thoughtful, inventive,** or **knowledgeable**—you may be a *Brainy Friend.*

A brainy friend comes in handy when you need facts at your fingertips or when you're stuck with your homework. She's also swishy to have in your group for a school project!

Or you could be any combination of the above! What kind of friend is your best friend? What kind of friend do you think Emily is? How about Shona?

Top Tens

Have fun filling in your favorite things and finding out what your best friend likes as well.

MY TOP-TEN FAVORITE THINGS

1. Color: Neon Yellow
2. Book: Monkey and me
3. Animal: Dog / Elephant
4. Outfit: My soccer uniform
5. Celebrity: Taylor Swift
6. Movie: Frozen / ET
7. TV program: Castle
8. Music group: 1 Direction
9. Song: Roars, Roar, Frozen
10. Food: Pizza

It's OK to have more than one favorite—list as many as you can fit!

MY BEST FRIEND'S TOP-TEN FAVORITE THINGS

1. *Color:* blue

2. *Book:* Life of Pi

3. *Animal:* Dog / Elephant

4. *Outfit:* Christmas PJs

5. *Celebrity:* Sandra Bullock

6. *Movie:* Despicable Me / ET

7. *TV program:* Modern Family

8. *Music group:* Dave Matthews Band

9. *Song:* Somewhere Over Rainbow

10. *Food:* Pizza

Pair Profiles

Beside me, I could almost feel Shona's thoughts, the same as mine, weaving in between my own words.

Emily and Shona are alike in some ways, different in others. What about you and your best friend? Look at the questions below, and see if you fit any of the pair profiles.

* Do you:
    * wear the same type of clothes?
    * style your hair in the same way?
    * have the same interests?
    * like the same subjects at school?

* Have you filled in the same favorites in your top-ten lists?

* Do people sometimes mistake you for sisters—or even twins?

If you answered YES to most of these questions, then you're a *Peas-in-a-Pod Pair.*

It's swishy to have a friend who is so similar to you—you always want to do the same things, and you never argue.

Or maybe you like doing lots of
the same things together but have
hot and cold tempers.

* Does one of you get angry
  quickly, while the other
  stays calm?

* Does one of you shout and scream,
  while the other smoothes things over?

* Does one of you argue back if she thinks she's
  in the right, while the other is happy to agree
  to differ?

If you answered YES to most of the questions, then
you're a *Fire-and-Water Pair.*

While Fire is hot-tempered, Water is cool and calm.
When Fire gets overheated, Water helps to cool her
down. And if Water is too laid-back, Fire gets her
going!

Everyone's surprised that you're such good friends,
because you're as different as can be. Life is certainly
never boring if you're Fire and Water!

Perhaps you bring out
the best in each other,
even though you're as
different as day and night:

You can
always agree
that you're
best friends.

* Does one of you smile
  a lot, while the other
  looks more serious?

* Does one of you make friends quickly,
  while the other takes longer?

* Is one of you very chatty, while the
  other is quieter?

* Does one of you rush into things, while
  the other takes time to make plans?

If you answered YES to most of the questions, then you're a *Sun-and-Moon Pair.*

While Sun is cheerful and sunny-natured, Moon is quieter and more thoughtful. Sun brings lots of laughter to Moon's life, while Moon makes Sun stop and think about things—just once in a while!

With Sun-and-Moon friends, there's always lots to discuss and new things to discover.

A Best Friend . . .

never forgets to tell her friend how important she is.

"And thanks," I added. "For everything. You're the bestest best friend anyone could want."
Shona's eyes shone brighter in the darkness.
"You are, you mean."

Secrets, Wishes, and Worries

Shona longs to be a siren someday. What do you wish for, and what do you worry about? Do you have a secret that you'll share only with your very best friend? Fill in your answers and have your best friend fill in hers.

ME

My secret ambition: ....

What I want for my birthday: I Phone ....

My biggest worry: I won't have any friends

If I could have three wishes, they would be:

Wish 1: To have a better life

Wish 2: To be nicer and not bossy

Wish 3: To not say something I didn't mean to.

My biggest secret: ....
....

A Best Friend . . .
always keeps your secrets safe.

Can you keep a secret?
Everybody has secrets, of
course, but mine's different,
and it's kind of weird.
— *Emily*

When you've filled in your secrets, make sure you hide this book somewhere safe!

MY BEST FRIEND

My secret ambition: ....

What I want for my birthday: ....

My biggest worry: ....

If I could have three wishes, they would be:

Wish 1: ....

....

Wish 2: ....

....

Wish 3: ....

....

My biggest secret: ....

....

PART II

Friendship and Fun

I made my way to Rainbow Rocks and hung around at the edge of the water, keeping hidden from the shore. A minute later, Shona arrived.

"You're here!" She grinned, and we dipped under. She took me in a new direction, out across Shiprock Bay. When we came to the farthest tip of the bay, Shona turned to me. "Are you ready for this?" she asked.

"Are you joking? I can't wait!"

She flipped herself over and started swimming downward. I copied her moves, scaling the rocks as we swam deeper and deeper.

What Do You Wear?

Your clothes cover you up, but they're also very revealing. What you wear says a lot about you—unless your mom chooses all your clothes for you! Take a peek inside your closet, and check out your best friend's style, too.

Do you love to wear:

* pretty pastel colors?

* frills and bows?

* plenty of sparkle, glitter, and twinkly sequins?

* floaty skirts, beautifully beaded flip-flops, and soft, fluffy cardigans?

YES? Then you're a *Gorgeous Girl.*

You've got lots in common with Emily's best friend, Shona. You love being a girl and looking pretty, and you enjoy buying new clothes and trying out different outfits. Like Shona, you always like to look your best.

Or do you love to wear:

　　✳ Spandex and stretchy clothes you can move in?

　　✳ sneakers and tracksuits?

　　✳ hooded sweatshirts and athletic shorts?

　　✳ sweatbands instead of bracelets?

YES? Then you're a *Sporty Star.*

You wear a team uniform rather than clothes, and you probably love sports, whether it's jogging, gymnastics, or kicking at people's ankles in soccer. Or maybe you just like chilling out in your cozy sweat suit.

Or do you love to wear:

  * jeans and combat boots?

  * cool tops and T-shirts?

  * high-tops and other trendy sneakers?

YES? Then you're a *Casual-Cool Chick.*

You're a laid-back and relaxed sort of girl who isn't too hung up on how she looks. You know how to look good—without looking as though you've tried too hard.

Or do you love to wear:

* whatever you like?

* a mix of all sorts of styles?

* anything—as long as it's fresh and funky?

YES? Then you're definitely a *Trendsetter*.

There's no way you're going to conform, because it's you who sets the trends! You're the sort of girl who likes to stand out from the crowd—in more ways than one!

She swam toward me, clutching her tote bag against her side. It was silver and gold and covered in tiny pink shells. Shona always had the prettiest things. She was the kind of mermaid you imagine mermaids to be, all girly and sparkly, with shiny long blond hair.

Handwriting Revelations

Did you know that your handwriting says a lot
about the sort of person you are? The study of
handwriting is called graphology, and it can be
taken very seriously—but this guide is just for fun.

Here is some space for you to write a few sentences
so that you can take a good look at your handwriting.

MY WRITING

I Love dogs.
I LOVE SOCCER.
I hate pigs.
Yay

Now, have your best friend write in the box below. Then turn the page to see what your handwriting reveals about each of you.

It doesn't need to be your best handwriting, just your normal, everyday style.

MY BEST FRIEND'S WRITING

....
....
....
....
....
....
....
....
....
....

THE SLOPE OF YOUR WRITING

Is your writing upright? Or does it slope to the left or to the right? Here's what it means:

Upright: *You can stand up for yourself.*

Right slope: *You're friendly and talkative.*

Left slope: *You're sometimes shy and secretive.*

SIZE

How big is your writing compared to your friend's?

Big and bold: *You're probably outgoing and confident.*

Small: *This suggests that you're fairly quiet and probably do well at school.*

PRESSURE

Did you press hard when you wrote, or is your writing fairly faint?

Hard pressure: *You take things seriously.*

Light pressure: *You're sensitive and kind to others.*

STROKES

If your upward strokes, like your *l*'s, *t*'s, and *h*'s are taller than most people's, this could mean that you aim high and are very ambitious.

Finally, look at your lower strokes, as in *g, p,* and *y:*

Short and straight: *You're sometimes impatient.*

Nice and rounded: *You're a gentle person.*

Look back at Emily's and Shona's handwriting, too, on pages 2–3, and see if you think their writing reflects their personalities.

Hair Know-How

It isn't just the clothes you wear or your handwriting that say lots about your personality, it's the way you wear your hair, too.

Look at the profiles below to see what your hairstyle reveals about you and your best friend.

* Do you like to wear your hair long, loose, and natural?

* Are you always so busy that you have no time for messing around with fussy hairstyles?

YES? You're a *Simply Natural Girl.*

You're full of energy and always on the go. You love the outdoors—especially the seaside, and you love animals, too. You'd love to gallop on a horse along a beach with the waves crashing and your hair blowing in the sea breeze.

* Do you like your hair out of the way,
  neatly tied back?

* Do you like to be able to concentrate on
  what you're doing—whether it's sports
  or studying?

YES? You're an *In-Control Chick.*

You're serious and determined. Either you're
studying hard, with your head in a book, or you're
sporty, with your eyes fixed firmly on the ball.

*"I like your cap," I said, and smiled back as she
squashed her hair into her tight, pink swimming
cap. I squeezed my ponytail into mine. I usually
wear my hair loose; Mom made me put it in a
scrunchie today. My hair is mousy brown and
used to be short, but I'm growing it out right
now.*

* Do you like experimenting
  with your hair?

* Does your hair always
  look different and
  eye-catching?

**Make sure
to brush your
hair often, or it
could get totally
tangled!**

YES? You're a *Crazy Creative*.

You're original and inventive. Your twists might
turn into tangles, and your hairdos might be hair-
don'ts, but you make an impact wherever you go
with your flamboyant style and big personality.

34

* Does your hair look as if it hasn't seen a brush for days?

* Does your mom despair and suggest that there might be a bird's nest on your head?

YES? You're a *Hair Horror.*

You're such a live wire and so busy doing lots of exciting things that you don't have time to worry about your hair.

If you want to experiment with a new look, try out different ways to do your hair. It's an easy and fun way to change your appearance. Just grab a brush and start styling!

I was trying to grow my hair, and it was past my shoulders now, but it still never looked anything like Shona's: sleek and beautiful and, well, mermaidlike, I guess.

Friendship Mobile

This fabulous friendship mobile is a lovely way to display all the mementos you and your best friend have collected together.

You'll need:

* cardboard or thick construction paper

* scissors

* glue

* crayons, markers, paints, or glitter (optional)

* ribbon or string

* beads and sequins

* clear adhesive tape

* a pretty coat hanger or a paper plate

* mementos that are important to you and your best friend, such as photographs, tickets from movies you've seen together, notes you've written to each other, birthday cards you've exchanged, pictures you've drawn, or poems you've written together

How to do it:

1. Cut the cardboard or construction paper into shapes to stick the mementos onto. You could make the shapes square, round, heart-shaped, or even starfish-shaped.

2. Glue each memento onto each cut-out cardboard or construction-paper shape.

3. Decorate each shape with crayons, paints, or markers.

4. Cut pieces of string or ribbon. You can make these the same length—or all different lengths, if you like.

5. Thread beads onto the strings to make your mobile pretty. (You could add separate strings of beads to make it even swishier.)

6. Tape one end of the string or ribbon to the back of each paper shape. If you don't like seeing the tape when the shapes twist and turn on the mobile, glue another piece of cardboard or paper onto the back of each one so that it covers the tape.

7. Tie the other ends of the ribbon to the coat hanger (or to a paper plate; see below) to make your mobile. Space the ribbons out so that you can see all the mementos.

To hang mementos from a paper plate instead of a coat hanger:

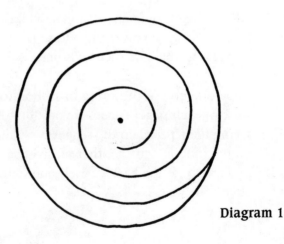

This mobile looks wonderful spinning and twirling in the breeze.

1. Draw a spiral on the paper plate, as shown in diagram 1, and cut along the line.

Diagram 1

2. Decorate the plate with sequins or glitter.

3. Tape your ribbons or strings to the plate, along with one central ribbon to hang the mobile up, as shown in diagram 2.

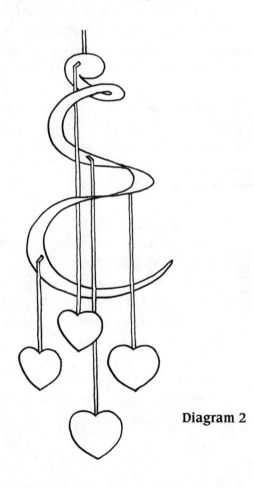

Diagram 2

Fun on the Beach

A second later, her tail was sticking up. Not twisting around madly like mine did, more as if she were dancing or doing gymnastics. In the moonlight, her tail glinted like diamonds.

When she came back up, I clapped. Or tried to anyway, but I slipped back under when I lifted both arms out and got water up my nose.

If you and your best friend visit the beach, there are lots of great things you can do together, even when it's too cold to swim in the sea.

Here are a few ideas:

* Instead of sand castles, why not try making a sand sculpture? Collect pebbles, shells, and seaweed to decorate your sculpture, too. Try making a turtle with a round shell patterned with pebbles, an octopus with big shell eyes and strands of seaweed for tentacles, or a mermaid with a shell bikini and seaweed hair.

* If the sand is firm, try making a little "sandman," just as you'd make a snowman. Don't forget to give him a hat so he doesn't get sunburned!

* If the sand is too
soft for a sculpture,
try making a flat piece
of artwork. Collect lots
of pebbles, shells, and
seaweed, and see if you can
make an amazing picture or collage.

Be sure to take a photo before the sea washes your sculpture away.

* Have a stone-skipping contest with your
friend. Collect a handful of flat, smooth
stones and take turns skipping them. Count
up your total number of skips and see who
gets the most.

Tip: If your stones are plopping into the water,
you're throwing them up too high, and if they're
whizzing straight in without skipping, you're
throwing too low. Hold the stone flat between
your thumb and finger. Move your hand forward,
and just before releasing the stone, quickly flick
your wrist. Some people get the knack right
away—if you don't, keep practicing!

Sea-Creature Feature

A pair of golden sea horses weaved their way around long trails of reeds that swayed and dipped in the current, their tails entwined. Gangs of paper-thin fish with bright yellow tails and round-bellied blue fish with black eyes all darted purposefully around me.

Emily and Shona swim with all sorts of strange sea creatures. Just for fun, imagine that some of these creatures were human! What sorts of personalities would they have? Which of these descriptions most closely resemble you and your best friend?

A.
You take life as it comes and have an easygoing nature. You're cool and calm, but you react quickly if you're in danger. And you have a sharp tongue if someone upsets you.

B.
You appear to be tough and argumentative on the outside, but you're really rather shy and sensitive. In fact, deep down, you're a great big softy.

C.

You're friendly and popular, and even though you spend lots of time messing around with your friends, you always do really well at school.

D.

You're gentle and quiet and a good, loyal friend. You take life at an easy pace, but you do like to know everything that's going on.

E.

You lose your temper and get into arguments quickly. And you always like to be the winner.

When you've decided whether you're most like A, B, C, D, or E, go to the next page and see what sort of sea creature you most resemble.

Sea-Creature Feature
ANSWERS

A. You're a *Jellyfish*.
Just like you, a jellyfish is a laid-back creature, drifting slowly and silently through the sea. But if danger threatens, its reactions are as quick as lightning. When you're attacked, you fight back with your sharp tongue, while a jellyfish fights back with its painful sting.

B. You're a *Sea Urchin*.
You protect your sensitive soul with a tough front, and a sea urchin does just the same. Its body is actually very soft inside its shell, but the only part a sea urchin displays to the world is its outer covering of spiky spines.

C. You're a *Dolphin*.
Dolphins are lovable, and so are you. Just like you, a dolphin is very sociable and boisterous and enjoys lots of playful fun. Since dolphins are also considered to be one of the most intelligent animals, they'd definitely be near the top of the class if they went to school.

D. You're a *Sea Horse*.

These small and graceful creatures never make a sound, and they are very loyal to each other, so if you're a quiet and reliable sort of person, this is your closest match. Sea horses never hurry anywhere, but they are very watchful, with highly mobile eyes to notice predators.

E. You're a *Shark*.

If you're short-tempered and sometimes enjoy a fight, you must be a shark. Sharks can be dangerous, so let's hope this isn't like you (or your best friend, either)!

Polish Up on Jewelry

The rock was covered with a collection that lit up the classroom, splashing a hundred colors all around us. I stared at it. Seaweed in bright pinks and greens, shells with the prettiest swirling patterns, sea flowers of every color, ancient jars filled with sand so bright it was more like glitter. Bright blue and green and orange crystals, shining white rocks.

Emily and Shona's class collected jewels from the sea, then laid out their treasure on the rocks for everyone to view. Why don't you and your best friend lay out your jewelry too and see what it reveals.

Delicate
Is your friend's jewelry dainty and pretty, to match her girly clothes? Is her jewelry box full of sparkly bangles, glittery necklaces, and delicate rings? Then she sounds like a sweet friend, and you love going shopping with her to check out the latest styles.

Chunky
Maybe your friend prefers her jewelry chunky and colorful? Does she love great big rings, bold bracelets, and showstopping pendants? She's definitely someone who likes to be noticed. She's probably outgoing and dramatic, with a personality as big as her bangles!

46

Unusual

Does your friend like her
jewelry to be completely
different? Maybe sometimes
she even makes her own—so
that no one can copy her and it's
always unusual and unique. Her choice
of jewelry shows that she's a brave person,
because it takes a lot of courage to be a true individual.

Cover a plain box with shells to make a swishy mermaid-style jewelry box.

Precious

Does your friend's jewelry box just contain a few
treasured pieces? Maybe she has a special present from
you in there, or a family heirloom—perhaps a locket
or a ring? Does she wear them only occasionally and
always make sure that they are safe? Her jewelry
might not be expensive—but it's precious to her,
and this shows that she's loyal, trustworthy, and a
caring and thoughtful friend.

*I turned over one final stone and there it was,
glinting at me, throwing light in a multicolored
arc all around. I gasped.*

*A ring. A thick gold band with the biggest,
brightest diamond I had ever seen in my life.*

Friendship Bracelets

Friendship bracelets are a great gift to make and swap with your best friend.

You'll need:

* different colors of embroidery thread

* scissors

* tape

* small beads and a needle (optional)

How to do it:

1. Choose three colors of thread, and cut two strands of each color about 18 inches long. (You can use just one strand of each color, but the bracelet will be very thin.)

2. Tie all six threads together with a knot at the top.

3. Tape the knotted end to something firm and flat, like a table or clipboard.

> **Use thread and beads in shades of green and blue, like the colors of the waves.**

4. Now, grasping the two strands of each color at a time, start braiding—just as you'd braid your hair. If you're not sure how to do this, follow the "How to Braid" instructions on the next page.

5. Thread beads on as you braid to make the bracelet even prettier.

6. When the bracelet is long enough to go around your friend's wrist with some length to spare, make a knot in the end.

7. Trim the ends to neaten it up.

8. Wrap the bracelet around your friend's wrist, and tie the two knotted ends together.

HOW TO BRAID

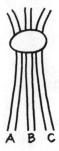
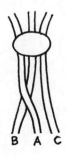
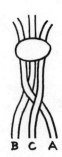

A   B   C   B   A   C   B   C   A

1. Starting position: Use two strands each of three different colors of thread.

2. Take the left two strands of thread (A) and pull them to the right, crossing over the center two strands (B).

3. Take the right two strands of thread (C) and pull them to the left, crossing over the two strands that are now in the center (A).

Then go back to the left two strands of thread (now B) and pull them to the right, crossing over the two new center strands (C).

Repeat this until you've made a braid.

Style Files

Now look back at pages 12–13 (Personality Profiles), 24–27 (What Do You Wear?), 32–35 (Hair Know-How), 44–45 (Polish Up on Jewelry), and 16–19 (Pair Profiles) and complete your style files. Which categories do you and your best friend have in common? Do you think your appearance reflects what you're really like, or are you disguising your true personality?

MY STYLE FILE

Personality profile: Adventurous Friend

Clothes: Pretty Pastel colors

Hair: In control Chick

Jewelry: Dolphin

MY BEST FRIEND'S STYLE FILE

Personality Profile: ....

Clothes: ....

Hair: ....

Jewelry: ....

OUR PAIR PROFILE

....

Best Friends' Treasure Trove

You'll need:

* a shoe box

* treasures to put in it — see ideas on next page

* tape

* paint, or colored paper and glue (optional)

How to do it:

1. Decorate the box—paint it or glue on colored paper in your own special design.

2. Write both of your names on the front and the date that you created the treasure trove.

Keep a note of your ceremony date handy so you won't forget to keep your promise.

3. Decide together on a date for your special opening ceremony. It could be in a year's time or even longer, but make a promise to each other that you'll both be there.

4. On the outside, write *Not to be opened until . . .* and add the date you've agreed on.

5. When you've finished designing your treasure trove, it's time to find some special items to put inside. Think about what treasure you'd like to find when you open up the box again.

Here are a few ideas to get you started:

* Photographs of you and your best friend as you both look now.

* Pictures you've drawn of each other—or self-portraits, if you prefer—so you can see how your artistic talents as well as your appearance change over time.

* The latest issue of your favorite magazine.

* Some important news stories cut out of the paper.

* Your top-ten favorite things—you could copy what you've written in this book on pages 14–15.

* A letter all about you and your friend and why you are best friends.

When you've filled your treasure trove, seal the top with lots of tape. Then hide it somewhere safe and dry, like under your bed or in the back of your closet until the date of your special opening ceremony finally arrives.

PART III

Underwater Sleepover

*A*s I swam around the rocks at the end of the bay, *the water became clearer and softer. It was like switching from grainy black-and-white film into color. The fat gray fish were replaced by stripy yellow-and-blue ones with floppy silver tails, long thin green ones with spiky antennae and angry mouths, orange ones with spotted black fins — all darting about purposefully around me.*

Plans and Preparations

If you're going to have a sleepover or a party, why not give it an underwater theme? To help it all go smoothly, make sure to plan ahead!

SLEEPOVER PLANNING CHECKLIST

Date of sleepover: . . . .

Invitations ☐

Food ☐

Room decorations ☐

Activities ☐

Names of guests invited: *Attending?*

. . . . ☐

. . . . ☐

. . . . ☐

. . . . ☐

. . . . ☐

. . . . ☐

INVITATIONS

You can have lots of fun making invitations for your underwater sleepover. Here are some ideas to make them wonderfully watery.

* Draw pictures of mermaids on your invitations, and decorate their tails with sequins.

* Make sea-life-shaped invitations—fish, starfish, shells, or sea horses.

* Sprinkle your invitations with blue and green glitter so that they shimmer like the sea on a sunny day.

* For an extra-special sleepover, try making a sand-picture invitation (see page 62).

We weaved in and out of spaghetti-fringed tubes and swam into bushes with tentacles that opened wide enough to swim inside.

ROOM DECORATIONS

Use your imagination to decorate your bedroom and turn it into a stunning underwater seascape. If you have most of your decorations hanging from the ceiling, it will leave plenty of floor space for you and your friends.

* Cut strips of green crepe or tissue paper and tape them to the ceiling so that they hang down like seaweed.

* Blow up lots of blue balloons. Hang some from the ceiling, and scatter the rest around your room.

* Set out a table for sleepover snacks. Cover it with netting material, and decorate it with shells.

* Stencil shell and starfish shapes onto paper, cut out, and hang on the walls around your room.

FOOD

Just because you're having an underwater sleepover doesn't mean that all the food has to be fishy! Here's a variety of mouthwatering snacks:

* Tasty tuna sandwiches cut into fish shapes

* Pita bread or breadsticks, carrot and celery sticks, and a selection of delicious dips

* Bowls of chips, nuts, and pretzels

* Slices of pizza and chunks of garlic bread

* Homemade cookies—Yum!

* Jell-O "jellyfish"—make and chill Jell-O in individual cups. Then turn them upside-down on a plate—jellyfish!

Decorate your Jell-O jellyfish with licorice "tentacles."

A huge shoal of fish that had been sheltering in a cave suddenly darted out as one, writhing and spinning like a kaleidoscope pattern.

ACTIVITIES

Treasure Hunts

If you've got a few friends coming to your sleepover, why not start with a treasure hunt in your house or yard? Before your guests arrive, hide a box of treasure — full of yummy midnight snacks! Then choose the type of treasure hunt you want to have:

* Tell your friends that the treasure is hidden deep at the bottom of the sea. As they search your house or yard, tell them how deep (close) or shallow (far) they are, depending on how close they're getting to the treasure.

* Prepare a picture treasure hunt in advance. Hide a trail of pictures, each of which is a clue to the next hiding place. Give your friends the first clue, and watch them find their way to the final hiding place.

* You could have a picture treasure hunt with a mermaid theme. Collect a bikini top, a hand mirror, a hairbrush, a large shell, a tiara, and your *Emily Windsnap* books. Place each item around the house or yard. Then prepare your picture clues, and place them with the mermaid

objects. For the clues to your *Emily Windsnap* books, draw the front cover of each and see if your friends can guess which book to look in. Once again, the final clue leads to the treasure box full of tasty goodies.

For other activity ideas for your fun-filled sleepover, turn to page 65 for Total Transformations. By the end of the evening, you might not even recognize one another!

Then when you're all snuggled up in bed with your snacks, it's time to tell stories—you'll find some sea stories starting on page 86.

You could make up your own tales about mermaids or monsters of the deep.

Sand-Picture Invitations

These are eye-catching party or sleepover invitations you can make using colored sand. You can also just make a pretty sand picture with your friends! You do need to start well in advance, though, because the sand takes a few hours to dry after you've colored it. If you can't get any sand, you can use salt instead.

You'll need:

* sand (as fine as possible) or table salt

* plastic freezer or sandwich bags

* food coloring

* glitter

* newspaper or paper plates

* construction paper or cardboard

* pencil

* containers for the colored sand

* glue

* spoon

How to do it:

Keep your picture bold and simple!

1. First, color the sand: For each color, pour about half a cup of sand into a plastic bag and add 10–12 drops of food coloring.

2. Seal the bags, and knead the sand and food coloring together until the sand is evenly colored. If you want a darker color, add more food coloring and knead again.

3. Dry the sand out completely: Pour each color of sand onto a separate sheet of newspaper or a paper plate, and leave them all to dry in the sun or any warm, dry place.

4. While the sand is drying, draw your picture or pattern on a piece of construction paper or cardboard (try a smallish piece first—5 x 7 inches is a good size). Keep your pencil lines faint so that you won't see them on the finished picture. Don't forget to leave space on the card for words if you're making an invitation.

5. When the sand is dry, pour each color into a separate container. Old jam jars, cups, or plastic containers are all suitable.

6. Mix in some glitter if you want your picture to sparkle.

7. Decide which color you're going to use first, and where. Cover those parts of the paper with glue.

8. Now for the fun: using a spoon, sprinkle the colored sand over your picture. Shake the paper around until the sand has covered all the glue.

9. Leave for a few minutes to let the sand stick. Then gently shake the paper so that the loose sand falls off.

10. Continue with all the colors until every part of your picture is covered in colored sand.

A Best Friend . . .

always remembers your birthday.

Why not remember your friend's birthday by making her a beautiful present? Decorate a plain wooden picture frame by gluing on shells, and put in a photograph of the two of you having lots of fun together.

Total Transformations

But then, just below the white line that went across my tummy, I was someone else—something else. My suit melted away and, instead, I had shiny scales. My legs narrowed into a long, gleaming, purple-and-green tail, waving gracefully as I skimmed along in the water. I have to say that I had never done anything gracefully in my life, so it was kind of a shock! When I flicked my tail above the surface, it flashed an arc of rainbow colors in the moonlight.

Even if you and your friends can't transform yourselves into real mermaids the way Emily does, you can have fun at your sleepover by dressing up and totally transforming your image. What sort of look do you secretly admire but would never dare to wear? What would you like to be in your dreams? You might surprise your friends with your new look—and you might even discover a whole new you.

Turn the page for some new looks to try out— or make up your own!

MERMAID

If you dream of diving into the water and transforming into a beautiful mermaid, why not try the mermaid look?

How to get the look:

* Choose coordinating clothes and accessories—aim for sea greens and blues.

* Wear a bikini top—in a shimmery fabric if possible.

* Add a long, flowing skirt.

* Wear your hear long and loose: if you've got short hair, try a wig or clip-on extensions.

* Spray your hair with blue or green glitter hair spray.

* Accessorize with a shell necklace.

* Try a blue or green glittery eye shadow, or add swirls of similar glittery face paint to your face, shoulders, and arms.

* Go barefoot, or wear flip-flops.

GOTH GIRL

If you dream of being dark and dramatic and like
the idea of a gothic look, you might like to try this
wicked transformation.

How to get the look:

* Dress head to toe in black or dark purple.

* Whether your hair is long or short, you can back-
comb it into a funky, punky style. Just hold up
sections of your hair and run your comb down
through it toward the roots to make it stick out.
Use hair spray to help it stay in place.

* For a pale and ghostly look, use white face paint
or powder.

* Outline your eyes in black, and paint your lips
black or very dark red.

* For an especially spooky look, you could draw
a spiderweb on one cheek.

* Paint your nails black or dark purple. Or paint
them white, then draw on spiderwebs with black
nail polish using a toothpick or a fine paintbrush.

GLITTER GIRL

If you don't often get dressed up, why not go over-the-top for once? This is an attention-grabbing look, perfect for a party or girly get-together.

How to get the look:

* Wear a jazzy wig, or spray your hair with glitter hair spray.

* Add lots of sparkly hair accessories.

This is a good party look if you like to get noticed!

* Use shimmery face paint or makeup on your cheeks and eyes.

* Paint your nails with glossy nail polish.

* Wear your most outrageous jewelry—don't hold back!

* Wear a T-shirt with a silver or gold design or logo.

* Add some glittery jeans or a skirt.

* And if you own sparkly shoes, wear those too!

ROCK STAR

Do you secretly dream of being in a rock band one day? Here's how to look as though you already are.

How to get the look:

* Wear tight jeans, or a miniskirt and leggings.

* Add your coolest T-shirt, or a dressier top — a silky or lacy blouse — to contrast with the jeans in true rock-star style!

* Wear trendy boots or sneakers.

* Add a dramatically long coat.

* Add some pizzazz with a shiny belt or black velvet choker.

* For your makeup, emphasize your eyes with black or brown eyeliner.

* Tousled hair is a must, so make lots of loose braids in damp hair the night before. Then take out the braids and shake out your hair. If you don't have time for this, try some gentle back-combing — see Goth Girl — but aim for messy rather than spiky!

HAPPY HIPPIE

Perhaps you dream of wandering free, roaming the countryside in a caravan, or telling fortunes like Mystic Millie.

How to get the look:

* Your hair should be loose and free-flowing—but you could add in a few braids enhanced with colorful embroidery silk and adorned with beads and feathers.

* Wear long and flowing garments, layered skirts, tie-dyed T-shirts with flared sleeves, crazy-colored cardigans, loose vests, or anything velvet.

* Mix and match your color scheme—you shouldn't look neat and coordinated.

* On your feet try big boots, clompy sandals, or pretty beaded flip-flops.

* Go crazy with jewelry. Wear jangly beads and bracelets, long pendants, dangly earrings—the more the better.

* Add some brightly colored blue or purple eyeliner, and paint stars and moons on your cheeks.

Shona and I made bangles and necklaces from the shells we'd picked up, wove the fans into hats, stuck shiny stones in patterns on our tails and surrounded them with swirling patterns made from glittery pink sand.

PART IV

Beneath the Waves

*E*verywhere I looked, people were swimming this way and that. And they all had tails! Merpeople! Hundreds of them! There were mermaids with gold chains around slinky long tails, swimming along with little merchildren. One had a merbaby on her back, the tiniest little pink tail sticking out from under its sling. A group of mermaids clustered outside one passageway, talking and laughing together, bags made from fishing nets on their arms. Three old mermen sat outside a different tunnel, their tails faded and wrinkled, their faces full of lines, and their eyes sparkling as they talked and laughed.

"Welcome to Shiprock — merfolk style!" Shona said.

Ten Fascinating Facts about Mermaids

1. In French, *la mer* means "the sea." So the word *mermaid* means "maid of the sea."

2. A *merrow* is an Irish mermaid, but instead of a tail, she has webbed hands and feet.

3. Female merrows are said to be beautiful, but the males are green in color with red eyes and pig ears!

4. Cornish mermaids are called merrymaids— but they aren't merry; they're very moody! When they're in a good mood, they happily rescue sailors from drowning, but when they're in a bad mood, they help them to drown.

5. The *ningyo* is a monstrous Japanese mermaid, which is described as a human-headed fish.

6. If you eat the flesh of the *ningyo,* it's said that you'll live forever.

7. A Japanese legend says that mermaids do not cry wet, salty tears like ours; instead, they cry real pearls.

8. Oberon, King of the Fairies in William Shakespeare's play *A Midsummer Night's Dream*, says that a mermaid's singing is so charming that it calms rough seas and makes stars shoot through the sky.

9. In the harbor of Copenhagen in Denmark, there is a statue of Hans Christian Andersen's "little mermaid" character, based on his story of the same name.

You can read two extracts from "The Little Mermaid" on pages 92–96.

10. There's a plant called water silk that is also known as mermaid tresses, because when the thin strands float to the surface, they look like the long, flowing hair of a mermaid.

Two silhouetted mermaid figures gliding along below the surface, our shadows came and went, appearing briefly before suddenly growing distorted with the splash of a tail breaking the water's still surface.

Mermaid School

Before Emily met Shona, she attended Brightport Junior High and didn't even know that mermaids went to school. But then she discovered that there are schools just for mermaids and that they aren't at all like the schools she was used to attending.

"I was practicing for Beauty and Deportment," she said, *as if I totally would know what she was talking about. "We've got a test tomorrow, and I can't get my posture right. You have to sit perfectly, tilt your head exactly right, and brush your hair in a hundred smooth strokes. It's a pain in the gills trying to remember everything at once."*

In fact, everything is different at mermaid school — the classrooms . . .

Everyone began to take their seats on the smooth round rocks that were dotted around the circular room. It reminded me of the three-hundred-and-sixty-degree dome at the Museum of Science movie theater, where they show films of daredevil flights and crazy downhill skiing. Only this wasn't a film — it was real!

the books…

I loved all my schoolbooks. They weren't like any schoolbooks I'd ever had before, that's for sure! For one thing, they were all made from the coolest shiny materials, or woven with seaweed and decorated with shells and pearls. And, for another, they were in the swishiest subjects! School had never been so much fun.

and especially the subjects!

I learned to dive with the grace of a dolphin and brush my hair like a real mermaid and sing the wordless songs of the sirens.

Here are some of the subjects in mermaid school:

* Beauty and Deportment

* Diving and Dance

* Aquatics and Animals

* Sailing and Stargazing

* Hair Braiding for Modern Mermaids

* Shipwreck Studies

Imagine your own perfect school—on land, under the sea, or somewhere completely different and amazing—where you can learn about anything you like, however weird and wonderful. Let your imagination run wild, think of the subjects you and your best friend would really enjoy, and design your very own dream schedule.

MONDAY
Morning: Soccer game
Afternoon: soccer goalie

TUESDAY
Morning: Soccer game
Afternoon: soccer goalie

WEDNESDAY
Morning: soccer game
Afternoon: Soccer goalie

THURSDAY
Morning: Soccer game
Afternoon: Soccer goalie

FRIDAY
Morning: soccer game
Afternoon: soccer goalie

A Best Friend . . .

is always big enough to apologize.

"I'm not surprised you're not speaking to me," I said, building up the courage to speak to her as we sliced through the water. Please don't ignore me, please!

Shona looked at me through heavy eyes. "What d'you mean?" she asked. "I thought you wouldn't be talking to me! I was so horrible to you. I've been a coward and a terrible friend. I wouldn't be surprised if you never want to speak to me again."

I grabbed her hand as we swam. "Shona, you weren't a terrible friend! If anyone was a terrible friend, it was me. I dragged you somewhere you didn't want to go."

Shona squeezed my hand. "I should never have let you take the blame. I'm so sorry," she said. ✳

Ten Sea-Life Snippets

1. The whale shark is the biggest fish in the world—
   it can be more than 50 feet long. Sounds terrifying!
   But actually, it eats only plants and plankton, and
   it wouldn't dream of eating people.

2. Sea horses are unique because it's the male that
   gives birth to the babies and takes care of them.
   A sea horse will usually keep the same partner all
   its life, and every morning the male and female
   perform a dance together to show their loyalty.

3. The fangtooth fish—also called an ogrefish—sounds
   scary and looks terrifying close-up with its huge
   jaw and teeth. But in reality, it's only a little fish,
   6 inches long at the most!

4. The deepest part of the sea, Challenger Deep in
   the Pacific Ocean, is 7 miles deep. If you were
   able to stand there on the bottom of the sea, the
   pressure of the water would be so strong that it
   would feel as though you were being squashed
   by ten elephants.

5. The largest-ever natural saltwater pearl was found
   off the Burmese coast. It weighs 6 ounces and is
   2½ inches in length.

6. The most famous shipwreck was that of the *Titanic,* which collided with an iceberg in 1912. Tragically, 1,503 people died.

7. The largest ocean carnivore ever seen was a great white shark more than 19 feet long. But scientists have found ancient fossilized jaws so enormous that they estimate the creature would have been more than 50 feet long. That's one very scary meat eater!

8. The tongue of a blue whale weighs as much as an elephant. Blue whales are the largest mammals, and they are also the loudest living things anywhere on the planet.

9. The Great Barrier Reef is the largest structure made by living creatures. The animals are called polyps, and they stick themselves together using a hard material called coral. The reef is home to hundreds of different types of brilliantly colored tropical fish, starfish, sea urchins, and sponges.

10. A type of sea urchin—the red sea urchin—is one of the longest-living animals. This small, spiny creature can live for more than two hundred years and never show any signs of aging!

Poetry Time

Mermaids and their mysterious world under the sea
are the perfect inspiration for poetry. What do you
and your best friend think of these beautiful poems?

From *The Mermaid*

Who would be
A mermaid fair,
Singing alone,
Combing her hair
Under the sea,
In a golden curl
With a comb of pearl,
On a throne?

I would be a mermaid fair;
I would sing to myself the whole of the day;
With a comb of pearl I would comb my hair;
And still as I comb'd I would sing and say,
"Who is it loves me? Who loves not me?"
I would comb my hair till my ringlets would fall.

—*Alfred, Lord Tennyson*

From **The Merman**

Who would be
A merman bold,
Sitting alone,
Singing alone
Under the sea,
With a crown of gold,
On a throne?

I would be a merman bold,
I would sit and sing the whole of the day;
I would fill the sea-halls with a voice of power;
But at night I would roam abroad and play
With the mermaids in and out of the rocks,
Dressing their hair with the white sea-flower;
And holding them back by their flowing locks
I would kiss them often under the sea,
And kiss them again till they kiss'd me
Laughingly, laughingly;
And then we would wander away, away,
To the pale-green sea-groves straight and high,
Chasing each other merrily.

— Alfred, Lord Tennyson

From *The Forsaken Merman*

Come, dear children, come away down.
Call no more.
One last look at the white-wall'd town,
And the little grey church on the windy shore.
Then come down.
She will not come though you call all day.
Come away, come away.
Children dear, was it yesterday
We heard the sweet bells over the bay?
In the caverns where we lay,
Through the surf and through the swell,
The far-off sound of a silver bell?
Sand-strewn caverns, cool and deep,
Where the winds are all asleep;
Where the spent lights quiver and gleam;
Where the salt weed sways in the stream;
Where the sea-beasts, ranged all round,
Feed in the ooze of their pasture-ground;
Where the sea-snakes coil and twine,
Dry their mail, and bask in the brine;
Where great whales come sailing by,
Sail and sail, with unshut eye,
Round the world for ever and aye?
When did music come this way?
Children dear, was it yesterday?

—*Matthew Arnold*

The Kraken

Below the thunders of the upper deep,
Far, far beneath in the abysmal sea,
His ancient, dreamless, uninvaded sleep
The Kraken sleepeth; faintest sunlights flee
About his shadowy sides; above him swell
Huge sponges of millennial growth and height;
And far away into the sickly light,
From many a wondrous grot and secret cell
Unnumber'd and enormous polypi
Winnow with giant arms the slumbering green.
There hath he lain for ages, and will lie
Battening upon huge sea-worms in his sleep,
Until the latter fire shall heat the deep;
Then once by man and angels to be seen,
In roaring he shall rise and on the surface die.

— Alfred, Lord Tennyson

85

Sea Stories

A chill gripped my chest as I realized I was
gliding over some dark rocks: hard, gray,
jagged boulders with plants lining every
crack. Fat gray fish with wide-open mouths
and spiky backs glared at me through cold
eyes. Long trails of seaweed stretched like
giant snakes along the seabed, reaching
upward in a clutch of leaves and stems.

Many myths and legends have been told about the
sea, some about mermaids, and others about selkies.
Selkies are sea fairies in the form of seals who are
able to shed their sealskins and appear as humans.
The following two stories are based on well-known
myths: the is about a mermaid who falls in love with
a human; the second is a lovely selkie legend.

The Mermaid of Zennor

Long ago, in the tiny Cornish village of Zennor, there
lived a man named Matthew who had a beautiful
singing voice. Every evening, he sang in the church,
built high on the rocky cliffs overlooking the sea.

One moonlit evening, a mermaid named
Morveren heard Matthew's wonderful singing, and
she left her watery home and crept ashore to listen.

When she returned to the sea, her father was furious.

"You must always stay hidden," he warned, "or the people will catch you and keep you as a prisoner."

So every evening, when Morveren returned to the shore, she did as her father had said and kept well out of the way. Day by day, Morveren grew more enchanted with Matthew's singing, and she fell deeply in love with him. And every day, she found it harder to hide away from the man she loved.

At last she could stand it no longer, and as Matthew and the villagers left the church, she slipped out from the shadows. When Matthew saw her, he was captivated by the mermaid's beauty. He picked her up in his arms and ran into the sea with her. Matthew's friends and family chased after him, but they weren't quick enough. They never saw Matthew or the mermaid again.

Some say that on a stormy night, you can still hear Matthew's voice singing from the depths of the sea, warning sailors of the dangers ahead.

The village of Zennor is a real place in Cornwall, and if you ever get the chance to visit, have a look in the church. There, carved in dark wood on the end of a bench, you'll find the Mermaid of Zennor with a comb and a looking glass in her hands.

The Selkies of Sanday

*M*any years ago, a young fisherman named Willie Westness was digging for bait in a small sandy bay when he heard a cry of pain from the rocks nearby. Willie left his digging and walked quietly toward the rocks where he found a female seal and her newborn pup.

The mother lumbered into the sea, but the pup lay helplessly at Willie's feet. He picked it up, and the soft little pup snuggled into his coat and nuzzled his hand. Willie thought the pup would make a good pet for his son, and he buttoned it up in his coat to take home.

Then he heard the cry again. The mother seal was wailing at the edge of the water.

"What was I thinking?" said Willie to the pup. "You belong in the sea with your mother." Gently, he laid the pup at the water's edge and watched until it was safely back with its mother.

Nine years later, Willie's three youngest children, Johnny, Jeannie, and little Tam, were exploring the same sandy bay. They clambered over the rocks and didn't notice that it was getting late and the tide was coming in fast. Before long, they were trapped, and every minute the sea grew deeper. Johnny waded out as far as he could to shout for help, but no one came, and Jeannie and Tam began to cry.

Suddenly two women wearing gray cloaks appeared as if from nowhere. "Come with me," said the older woman, smiling at them with her round brown eyes. She took Jeannie and Tam's hands, and holding them in her firm grasp, she led them around the rocks. The sea rose up to their necks, but they never once lost their footing, and they were soon back on the sand. The younger woman helped Johnny, and it wasn't long before he, too, reached the shore.

The children thanked the two kind women for their help, but the older woman shook her head. "No need to thank us," she said. "But be sure you say these words to your father: *One spared to the sea is three spared to the land.*"

The children ran to tell their father the woman's words. They looked back once to wave, but the gray-cloaked women were nowhere in sight—only two seals swimming slowly out to sea.

There are many scary legends about the sea, tales of monsters and ghostly shipwrecks, passed from one generation to the next. The legend of the Kraken was the subject of both Lord Tennyson's poem of that name (page 85) and Emily's adventures in *Emily Windsnap and the Monster from the Deep*.

The Kraken

And the kraken rose. It burst through the water, screaming up from deep below the surface, its long face stretched wide by angry, gaping jaws exposing daggerlike teeth as its tentacles scrambled madly like a mass of giant maggots, smashing the still surface of the sea. As we watched, the water fell away, pouring like a waterfall, leaving just the kraken, surrounded in its fury by utter, black emptiness.

Emily and Shona experience the horrors of the kraken. Fortunately, they live to tell the tale.

But does the kraken really exist? Evidence of a giant squid was first discovered in the nineteenth century, when men out hunting whales saw the scars of giant suckers on the bodies of the whales. It looked as though the whales had been in a fight with another creature—and it was obviously something large and fierce! Then pieces of tentacle, some as thick as a man's body, were found inside a dead whale's stomach.

And so the legend of the kraken grew. Terrible tales were told of sailors being eaten alive, and it was said that the kraken even attacked a ship. It was caught up in the propellers and chopped to pieces. But the biggest danger to ships was said to be the terrifying whirlpool that the kraken created when it descended back into the depths of the sea.

Spooky Ships

On stormy nights when the waves are smashing on the rocks, it's said that ghostly ships have been sighted, lit by a flash of lightning. According to folklore, the phantom crew are reliving—over and over again—the night that their ship was wrecked and they all plunged to their deaths. The crew of the most famous phantom ship, the *Flying Dutchman,* is said to be not only ghostly but ghastly, sailing the seven seas forever to bring doom and destruction to other ships.

The Little Mermaid

Hans Christian Andersen's famous story of another mermaid who falls in love with a human was first published in 1837 and has remained popular ever sense. The youngest of six sisters, the little mermaid was the most beautiful of them all, but she was quiet and thoughtful. More than anything, she longed to know more about the world of humans. When the little mermaid finally turned fifteen, she was allowed to visit the surface for the first time.

. . . So she said, "Farewell," and rose as lightly as a bubble to the surface of the water. The sun had just set as she raised her head above the waves; but the clouds were tinted with crimson and gold, and through the glimmering twilight beamed the evening star in all its beauty. The sea was calm, and the air mild and fresh. A large ship, with three masts, lay becalmed on the water, with only one sail set; for not a breeze stiffed, and the sailors sat idle on deck or amongst the rigging. There was music and song on board; and, as darkness came on, a hundred colored lanterns were lighted, as if the flags of all nations waved in the air. The little mermaid swam close to the cabin windows; and now and then, as the waves lifted her up, she could look in through clear glass window-panes, and see a number of well-dressed people within. Among them was a young prince, the most beautiful of all, with large black eyes; he was sixteen years of age, and his birthday was being kept with much rejoicing. The sailors were dancing on deck, but when the prince came out of the cabin, more than a hundred rockets rose in the air, making it as bright as day. The little mermaid was so startled that she dived under water; and when she again stretched out her head, it appeared as if all the stars of heaven were falling around her, she had never seen such fireworks before. Great suns spurted fire about, splendid fireflies flew into the blue air, and everything was reflected in the clear, calm sea beneath. The ship itself was so brightly illuminated that all the people, and even the smallest rope, could be distinctly and plainly seen. And how handsome the young prince looked, as he pressed the hands of all present and smiled at them, while the music resounded through the clear night air.

It was very late; yet the little mermaid could not take her eyes from the ship, or from the beautiful prince. The colored lanterns had been extinguished, no more rockets rose in the air, and the cannon had ceased firing; but the sea became restless, and a moaning, grumbling sound could be heard beneath the waves: still the little mermaid remained by the cabin window, rocking up and down on the water, which enabled her to look in. After a while, the sails were quickly unfurled, and the noble ship continued her passage; but soon the waves rose higher, heavy clouds darkened the sky, and lightning appeared in the distance. A dreadful storm was approaching; once more the sails were reefed, and the great ship pursued her flying course over the raging sea. The waves rose mountains high, as if they would have overtopped the mast; but the ship dived like a swan between them, and then rose again on their lofty, foaming crests. To the little mermaid this appeared pleasant sport; not so to the sailors. At length the ship groaned and creaked; the thick planks gave way under the lashing of the sea as it broke over the deck; the mainmast snapped asunder like a reed; the ship lay over on her side; and the water rushed in. The little mermaid now perceived that the crew were in danger; even she herself was obliged to be careful to avoid the beams and planks of the wreck which lay scattered on the water. At one moment it was so pitch dark that she could not see a single object, but a flash of lightning revealed the whole scene; she could see every one who had been on board excepting the prince; when the ship parted, she had seen him sink into the deep waves, and she was glad, for she thought he would now be with her; and then she remembered that human beings could not live in the water, so that when he got down to her father's palace he would be quite dead. But he must not die. So she swam about among the beams and planks which strewed the surface of the sea, forgetting that they could crush her to pieces. Then she dived deeply under the dark waters, rising and falling with the waves, till at length she managed to reach the young prince, who was fast losing the power of swimming in that stormy sea. His limbs were failing him, his beautiful eyes were closed, and he would have died had not the little mermaid come to his assistance. She held his head above the water, and let the waves drift them where they would.

In the morning the storm had ceased; but of the ship not a single fragment could be seen. The sun rose up red and glowing from the water, and its beams brought back the hue of health to the prince's cheeks; but his eyes remained closed. The mermaid kissed his high, smooth forehead, and stroked back his wet hair; he seemed to her like the marble statue in her little garden, and she kissed him again, and wished that he might live. Presently they came in sight of land; she saw lofty blue mountains, on which the white snow rested as if a flock of swans were lying upon them. Near the coast were beautiful green forests, and close by stood a large building, whether a church or a convent she could not tell. Orange and citron trees grew in the garden, and before the door stood lofty palms. The sea here formed a little bay, in which the water was quite still, but very deep; so she swam with the handsome prince to the beach, which was covered with fine, white sand, and there she laid him in the warm sunshine, taking care to raise his head higher than his body. Then bells sounded in the large white building, and a number of young girls came into the garden. The little mermaid swam out farther from the shore and placed herself between some high rocks that rose out of the water; then she covered her head and neck with the foam of the sea so that her little face might not be seen, and watched to see what would become of the poor prince.

What do you think happens to the little mermaid and her prince? You can read the rest of Hans Christian Andersen's story (be warned: you may need tissues!), or write your own ending on the pages that follow.

Writing Time!

If you and your best friend like writing, why don't you make up a poem or a sea story together?

* Imagine that you're a mermaid. What's it like living below the sea?

* You're on a voyage, and the ship crashes into the rocks. How do you survive?

* Remember a day at the beach that you really enjoyed.

* Describe a day in the life of your favorite sea creature—or the one you like least.

Then, on page 110, you can write all about your best friend—what fun adventures you've had, what you like about her, and how you met.

After you're done, have your best friend write all about you on page 118!

. . . .

. . . .

. . . .

. . . .

. . . .

. . . .

. . . .

. . . .

. . . .

. . . .

. . . .

. . . .

. . . .

My Best Friend . . .

....

....

....

....

....

....

....

....

....

....

....

....

....

These pages are for writing about your best friend and all the things you like about her.

....

....

....

....

....

....

....

....

....

....

....

....

....

....

....

....

....

....

....

....

....

....

....

....

....

....

....

....

My Best Friend . . .

....
....
....
....
....
....
....
....
....
....
....
....
....

Now let
your best friend
have a turn to
write about you!

·····································

·····································

·····································

·····································

·····································

·····································

·····································

·····································

·····································

·····································

·····································

·····································

·····································

·····································

·····································

·····································

....
....
....
....
....
....
....
....
....
....
....
....
....
....

....
....
....
....
....
....
....
....
....
....
....
....
....
....

Read all the
Emily Windsnap books!

Hardcover ISBN 978-0-7636-2483-5

Paperback ISBN 978-0-7636-2811-6

Hardcover ISBN 978-0-7636-2504-7

Paperback ISBN 978-0-7636-3301-1

Hardcover ISBN 978-0-7636-3330-1

Paperback ISBN 978-0-7636-3809-2

ISBN 978-0-7636-4060-6

The New York Times *best-selling series — now making a big splash as a boxed collection of all three enchanting mermaid adventures.*

Another magical adventure from Liz Kessler!

On sale now!

Hardcover ISBN 978-0-7636-4070-5

Philippa Fisher's Fairy Godsister

Philippa Fisher would like nothing more than a fairy godmother to grant her every wish. Still, she's taken aback when Daisy, the new girl at school, announces that she's Philippa's fairy god*sister,* since they're both the same age. Daisy's none too pleased with her new assignment, but she's obliged to grant Philippa three wishes. Now, if only Philippa would wish for something that made her life better, not worse!

Coming soon

Philippa Fisher and the Dream-Maker's Daughter
in September 2009!